Tra-la-la

Tra-la-la

Tra-la-la, tra-la-la

Tra-la-la, tra-la-la

EGMONT

We bring stories to life

This edition published in Great Britain 2008 by Dean
an imprint of Egmont UK Limited
239 Kensington High Street, London W8 6SA
© 2008 Disney Enterprises, Inc
Based on the Winnie-the-Pooh works by A. A. Milne and E. H. Shepard
Illustrations by Andrew Grey
Text by Jude Exley

ISBN 978 0 6035 6362 1
1 3 5 7 9 10 8 6 4 2
Printed in China

All About

Pooh

This book belongs to . . .

Meet Pooh

Here is Pooh, ready to be introduced to you.
Some of you may have met Pooh before, and you
may even think that you know him well.
You may know that Pooh's full name is

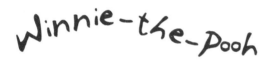

and even that he was once called
Edward Bear. But in this book,
you will learn all about the Best
Bear in All the World. And you
can listen to a story – just the kind of
story Pooh would like – a story about Pooh.
Because Pooh's that sort of bear . . .

A Poem about Pooh

Pooh is a Silly Old Bear

Who lives life without a care.

He's happiest when he has honey,

The taste of it makes him go funny,

Goloptious honey, sticky and runny!

That clever Bear of Little Brain,

Saved Piglet from the pouring rain!

There's nothing that he wouldn't do,

Life is fun with friends like you.

The Best Bear in All the World – Pooh!

Facts about Pooh

He was once called Edward Bear. But Christopher Robin changed his name to Winnie-the-Pooh, after a swan called Pooh, and a bear called Winnie.

He lives in the Forest. In case you ever want to visit, he lives under the name of Sanders. This isn't another name for Pooh, it is a sign by his front door.

He loves honey, and this sometimes causes problems – for Pooh. His favourite time for a little smackerel of something is 11 o'clock in the morning.

He makes up his own hums.
And poems and songs. It is rare that a day goes by without Pooh humming or singing a little song to himself.

He is a Bear of Very Little Brain.
Long words bother Pooh, and because of this, he finds it very difficult to understand Owl and Rabbit.

He sometimes has good ideas.
Like when he invented *The Floating Bear* and *The Brain of Pooh* to rescue Piglet from the flood.

He is a real friend.
When Eeyore lost his tail, Pooh found it. But, best of all, when Piglet lost his home, Pooh gave him a new one — with him!

He would sometimes like to be Kanga.
Pooh wishes he could jump like Kanga
and Roo. Every Tuesday, in the sandy part
of the Forest, he practises his
jumps with Kanga.

He discovered the North Pole.
Pooh went on an "expotition" to find the
North Pole. Roo fell into the river and Pooh
picked up the pole to rescue him.

He invented Poohsticks.
One day, Pooh dropped two fir cones in
the river to see which one would come out
 first. That was the beginning of the game
called Poohsticks, which Pooh invented.

In which we read about

Pooh

One day, Winnie-the-Pooh, or Pooh for short, was walking through the Forest when he heard a loud buzzing noise. Now, if there is one thing that Pooh knows about, it is buzzing noises. There is only one thing that makes a buzzing noise and that is a bee.

And there is only one reason why it makes a buzzing noise and that is because it has made some honey for Pooh to eat!

The
**buzzing
noise**

was

coming

from

the

top

of a

very

tall

tree.

So Pooh began to climb the tree, singing a little song to himself. "Isn't it funny, how a bear likes honey?"

He went higher . . . and higher . . . until he was just a few branches away, then . . .

crack!

Pooh said goodbye to the branch and bounced, crashed, spun and flew straight into a bush. Pooh brushed himself down and went to see his good friend, Christopher Robin, who lives in another part of the Forest.

Pooh had decided that what he really needed
was a blue balloon. He had thought about this very
carefully. If he had a blue balloon, he could pretend
to be a small black cloud in the sky, and then the
bees wouldn't realise that he wanted their honey.

Christopher Robin
didn't think that this would
work, but he decided to
help Pooh. So off they
went with a blue balloon.
Pooh rolled in mud
until he looked like a
small black cloud, or so
he thought, and then he held
on to the string and floated
up high into the sky.

But Pooh floated up metres away from the tree.
He could smell the honey. But he couldn't get to it.

"Do I look like a small black cloud in the
sky?" he asked.

"You look like a bear holding on to a balloon,"
replied Christopher Robin.

After a while, Pooh said in a loud whisper,
"I think the bees are
suspicious!"

So Pooh asked Christopher
Robin to walk up and down
with an umbrella saying that
it looked like it was about
to rain, just in case.

And, while Christopher Robin walked up and down, Pooh sang a song. And the bees all flew around him and one sat on his nose as he sang.

"Christopher Robin," called Pooh. "I have decided that these bees would make the wrong sort of honey, so I would like to come down. You must burst the balloon."

So Christopher Robin aimed very carefully at the balloon with a pea shooter, and the air came out very slowly and Pooh floated down to the ground. But he couldn't move his arms for days, and when a bee landed on his nose he had to blow it off.

A few days later, when Pooh was able to move his arms again to do his stoutness exercises, he made up a little hum as he stretched.

Tra-la-la, tra-la-la . . .

After breakfast, Pooh was walking through the Forest, humming his hum, hoping to share it with someone, when he came to a sandy bank. In the bank was a large hole.

"Rabbit lives inside that hole!" cried Pooh. "And that means someone to listen to my hum. And someone with food."

Pooh had realised that there were easier ways to get honey than pretending you were a small black cloud. But when Pooh called, Rabbit pretended that he wasn't at home. And even said that he was visiting Pooh!

"That's me," said a very surprised Pooh.

"Oh, come in then," said Rabbit.

So Pooh **squashed** and **squeezed** his way through the hole, and was very pleased when Rabbit asked him if he would like something to eat.

Pooh couldn't decide between honey or condensed milk, so he said **yes** to both.

After all, it was nearly eleven o'clock in the morning, and Pooh always liked a little something at that time of the day.

At last, after checking
that there was no food left,
Pooh thanked Rabbit with
a sticky voice, and said that he
must leave. He started to climb
out of the hole.
But he pulled and pushed, until his nose,
ears, front paws and shoulders were
in the open . . .

and then . . .

nothing . . .

"Oh, help and bother!" said Pooh.
"I can't move."

By now, Rabbit had gone out of his back door, and
round to the front to see Pooh.

"Give me your paws," he said, and Rabbit
pulled, and pulled, and pulled ...

"Ouch!" cried Pooh. He was stuck, and Rabbit knew why.

"I didn't like to say anything. But you've eaten too much," he said. "I shall see if Christopher Robin can help."

So, Rabbit brought Christopher Robin, who quickly saw that the there was only one thing to do.

"We'll have to wait for you to get thin again, so we can pull you out," he said.

Pooh was very anxious. He would have to stay there for a week without any food.

He began to sigh and then a tear rolled down his cheek.

"Would you read a sustaining story to help and comfort me?" he said.

"Of course, you Silly old Bear," said Christopher Robin.

And every day, he read to Pooh, while Pooh felt himself getting slimmer and slimmer.

Until, at the end of the week, Christopher Robin took hold of his front paws, and Rabbit and all his friends and relations took hold of Christopher Robin, and they pulled together.

With a sudden 'Pop!' they all fell
backwards and out came Pooh
— free at last.

He nodded to his friends and then
continued his walk
through the Forest,
humming proudly
to himself.

Tra-la-la.

Now, if there is one thing that Pooh missed when he was stuck in the hole, apart from honey, it was his friends.

Pooh enjoys spending time with his friends. And one very nice thing to do when you are with your friends is to play Poohsticks together.

One day, Pooh, Piglet, Rabbit and Roo were all playing Poohsticks at the bridge. The river was very lazy that day, so they had been leaning over the edge for a while, waiting to see whose stick would be first.

Roo kept thinking that he could see them, and had been very excited, but soon he was beginning to get bored by how long the sticks were taking. Until Pooh saw something.

"That's yours, Piglet," he said suddenly. "The grey stick coming out now."

Roo was very excited again, "Come on, stick!"

Piglet thought he might win and he squeaked excitedly, "Is it definitely mine?"

"It's grey.
And big.
Oh no,
it's
Eyore!"
said Pooh.

And there, floating in the river, with his legs in the air, was Eeyore!

"I didn't know you were playing Poohsticks, Eeyore," said Roo.

"I'm not. I'm waiting for someone to help me out of the river," he replied.

Everyone was silent, until Pooh said that he had
a sort of idea. Eeyore was already feeling unsure
about this idea.

"We could throw things into the river to wash
Eeyore on to the river bank," said Pooh.

Rabbit thought it was a very good idea. But Piglet
was worried that they might hit Eeyore by mistake,
and just then Pooh dropped the biggest stone he
could carry into the water. Splash!

And Eeyore disappeared ...

Even the sight of Piglet's stick coming under the bridge didn't cheer them up. But then Pooh saw something grey by the river bank – it was Eeyore, at last.

"Well done, Pooh," said Rabbit, kindly.

But Eeyore didn't thank Pooh. Instead he told Pooh that he had swum out of the way of the large stone he had thrown at him.

Pooh began to feel a bit anxious. He knew that his good ideas were often better in his brain than when they were out in the open.

But Eeyore was out of the river, and Pooh hadn't caused him any harm.

They all wanted to know how Eeyore had ended
up in the river.

"I was thinking by the river side when I was
bounced," he said.

And just as they were talking about being bounced,
who should come through the hedge, but Tigger.

"Hello," he said cheerfully.

Rabbit decided to ask Tigger exactly what had happened when he bounced Eeyore into the river.

"I was behind Eeyore when I coughed," said Tigger, making a rather surprising noise, which made little Piglet fall over.

"Now taking people by surprise like that is what I call bouncing," said Eeyore. "I was just minding my own business in my little corner of the Forest when Tigger bounced in it."

"I coughed," said Tigger crossly.

Just then, Christopher Robin walked towards the bridge, and the animals decided to ask him what he thought about it all.

"Well, I think," said Christopher Robin. "I think we should all play Poohsticks."

So that is exactly what they did. And Eeyore, who had never played Poohsticks before, won more games than anyone else.

As the afternoon passed, Rabbit took Roo home
to Kanga, and Tigger and Eeyore left together, leaving
Christopher Robin, Pooh and Piglet on the bridge
by themselves.

It was a quiet, peaceful summer afternoon in the
Forest, and for a long time they silently looked at the
river flowing beneath them.

Until Piglet said that he thought Tigger was all
right really.

"I don't suppose I'm right," said Pooh. "But I think
everyone is all right really."

And Christopher Robin agreed with the Silly old Bear.

Tra-la-la, tra-la-la

Tra-la-la

Tra-la-la

Tra-la-la

Tra-la-la

Tra-la-la

Tra-la-la